The Bone People Story

By Rhonda R. Reynolds

Illustrations by Ipan

D1602165

The Bone People Story

Paperback ISBN 979-8-218-24978-6

Text by Rhonda R. Reynolds
Illustrations by "Ipan" Arief N. Iffandy (https://www.etsy.com/shop/ipandyline)
Book design by Marc Schelske, Live210 Media

Special Thanks

IPan for his amazing illustrations and for being easy to work with. **Marc Schelske** for his knowledge and skills with publishing. Our son, **Skyler**, for his fascination with scary stories and for being the inspiration for this book. My husband of 50+ years, **Dennis**, for being my best friend and for his encouragement always. Grandchildren, **Cady** and **Mason**, for loving the story and Grammy becoming a published author. Our daughter, **Summer**, for being the driving force to get "The Bone People Story" published. Such a wonderful act of Love that means more than I can say. Thank you, Summer!

Dedicated to storytellers everywhere
who will give their best effort when their child or grandchild says
"tell me a story," with a look of absolute confidence that
a great story can emerge instantly.

History of The Bone People Story

Our son, Skyler, was about four years old and just learning to ride his bicycle with training wheels when I made up this story for him. We had driven to a country cemetery a few miles from our home in Beavercreek, Oregon, so he could ride his bicycle on the cemetery paths without worry of cars. He loved scary stories and would often ask me to make up a scary story for him.

As we sat on the cemetery bench eating our lunch, I had the idea to tell a story about the bone people coming out of their graves every night, only to disappear into their graves before daylight. Skyler liked the idea, so I kept going, unsure where the story would take us. When my story ended that day, I thought, "That was pretty good, if I do say so myself." I typed out the story as best I could recall when I got home and put it in a folder in my filing cabinet. I read it a few times but then forgot about it.

We raised our two children in Beavercreek and lived there for 33 years. When we became Empty Nesters, we decided to pack up and move to Netarts on the Oregon coast. We had to do a lot of downsizing. It was daunting, but we were excited to live on the coast, so we pressed ahead. As we settled into our new lifestyle and home, I remembered "The Bone People Story" and wondered where it might be. I was concerned it was lost forever.

One day I was going through our overstuffed filing cabinet, picking out documents to shred, when I noticed a folder titled "Rhonda's Writings." In that folder was "The Bone People Story" from so long ago. I was delighted! The next time our grandchildren visited, I read the story to them for the first time. Their enthusiasm reignited thoughts of publishing the story.

I attempted to draw illustrations myself, but to no avail, so my story returned to its folder for a few more years. Then, our daughter, Summer (who has had two books published herself) announced that she would help me get my story published. I was excited. She searched the internet for an illustrator and found Ipan. He has been great to work with. Summer and I had the best time fine-tuning our descriptions for Ipan and seeing what he came up with. We knew we had chosen the right illustrator when we saw the Bone People couple dancing and Ipan had the lady wearing a backless dress.

My husband, children, and grandchildren have been so supportive and encouraging of this story getting published. So I hope you enjoy it as much as my family has!

Once upon a time . . .

…there was a quiet little neighborhood cemetery just a few blocks from the center of town. It was always peaceful and pretty, with little winding paths and benches scattered here and there so people could rest and remember their loved ones who had passed.

What the townspeople didn't know was that every night, when it got really dark outside, the bone people would come out of their graves and have big parties. Some would sit on the benches or grave markers. Others would lie in the grass, or stroll around the grounds. Others would dance, or play tag with their bone friends.

But no matter how wonderful of a time the bone people were having, as soon as the sun began to rise, they would rush back into their graves. The cemetery would remain peaceful and quiet all of the daylight hours, and none of the townspeople ever suspected what was happening every night in the darkness.

One night, a young lady bone person named Bonnie and a young man bone person named David were sitting on a bench talking. Bonnie had died in a car crash, and David had died of cancer. Before the night was over, they fell in love. David asked Bonnie to be his wife. Bonnie was surprised and quickly said, "Yes." They found the bone person minister and asked him if he would marry them. He said he would. Everyone was so excited for the wedding.

On a beautiful warm summer evening, all the bone people gave Bonnie and David a lovely wedding with all the trimmings. Everyone had a wonderful time. When it started to get light outside, Bonnie went to David's grave with him. Her grave stayed empty from then on. They were very happy together.

Several months passed. At one of the nightly parties, Bonnie wasn't feeling well. David called for the bone people doctor. The doctor told them that Bonnie was pregnant! Bonnie and David were so surprised but happy and excited to be having a baby!

A few months later, on a warm spring evening, Bonnie gave birth to a beautiful baby girl. They decided to name her Belinda. Belinda was not like the bone people at all. She was a real live baby! Bonnie and David had a wonderful evening with their baby daughter but didn't stop to realize what having a real baby girl would mean at daybreak. As soon as it started to get light, Bonnie and David had to return to David's grave.

Since Belinda was a real live baby, she couldn't go with her parents and had to stay on top of the grave. Luckily, David's parents had left a small picnic quilt beside his grave on their last visit. Bonnie wrapped Belinda snuggly in the quilt, gave her a good night kiss, and laid her gently on the grass. Bonnie and David slipped sadly back into their grave but knew that David's parents would find Belinda very soon because they visited the cemetery early every morning.

Sure enough, only about an hour after Bonnie's good night kiss, David's parents arrived at the cemetery to put flowers on their son's grave. They were surprised to find a tiny baby girl wrapped in their picnic quilt lying on the grass beside David's grave. Before taking the baby home, they wrote a note and left it on their son's grave. They took her to the hospital, where the doctors said the baby girl was perfectly healthy.

When Bonnie and David came out of their graves that evening, they found John and Susan's note. Although they were sad that Belinda was gone, they were happy to know that David's parents were caring for their beloved baby, just as they had hoped. They knew Belinda would be safe and loved very much. The police searched and searched for clues about the baby girl's parents, but of course, they never found any.

David's parents took good care of baby Belinda and came to love her very much. Finally, David's Mom and Dad were permitted to adopt baby Belinda. Ever since their son had died, they had been very lonely and loved having a child to raise again. They never once suspected that their adopted daughter was really their granddaughter.

Certificate of Adoption

This certifies that
John & Susan Jones
have officially adopted
Baby Belinda.

By signing this certificate,
we promise to love and protect
Baby Belinda and help her live a
happy and healthy life.

John Jones

Susan Jones   May 14, 2023

Belinda grew into a lovely young woman. She fell in love and married her best friend, Peter Smith. They had children, then grandchildren, and even great-grandchildren. Belinda had a wonderful lifetime full of love and happiness, but she always wondered who her birth parents were and why they could never be found. Her adoptive parents had told her many times about the miracle of finding her on their son's grave wrapped in a picnic quilt.

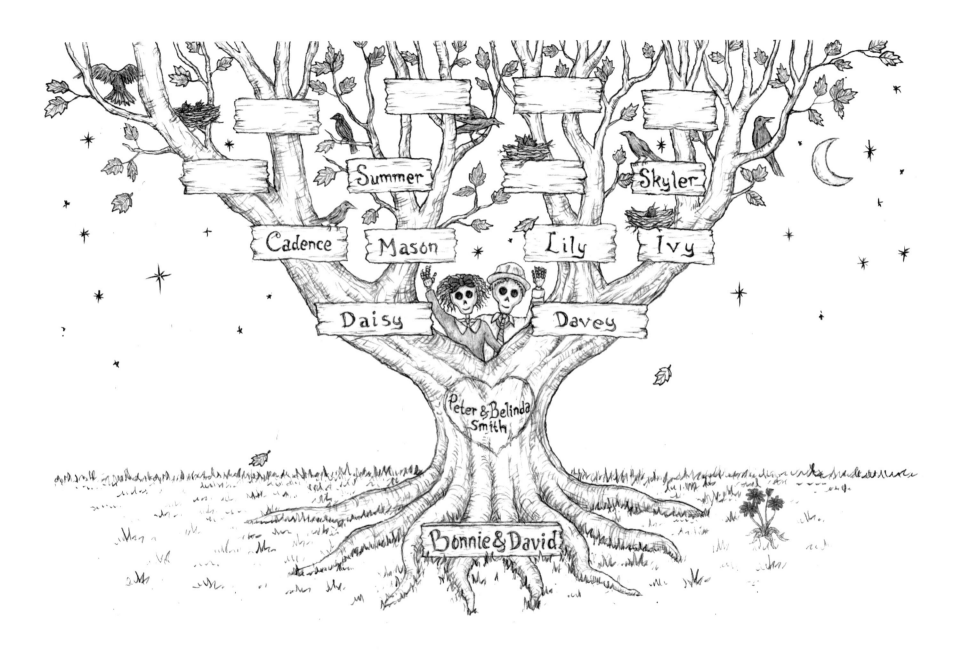

When Belinda was 83 years old, she died. All of Belinda's children, grandchildren, and great-grandchildren were very sad because they would miss her, but Bonnie, David, John, and Susan were overjoyed! They finally had their daughter back – but now she was a bone person, so they could all be together forever and ever.

Printed in the USA
CPSIA information can be obtained
at www.ICGtesting.com
JSRC072040200923
48731JS00002B/2